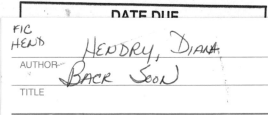

DATE DUE

FIC
HEND        HENDRY, DIANA
AUTHOR
            BACK SOON
TITLE

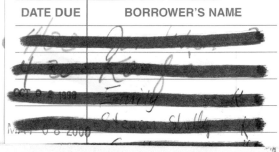

| DATE DUE | BORROWER'S NAME |
|---|---|
|  |  |
|  |  |
| OCT 0 2 1998 |  |
| MAY 0 8 2000 |  |

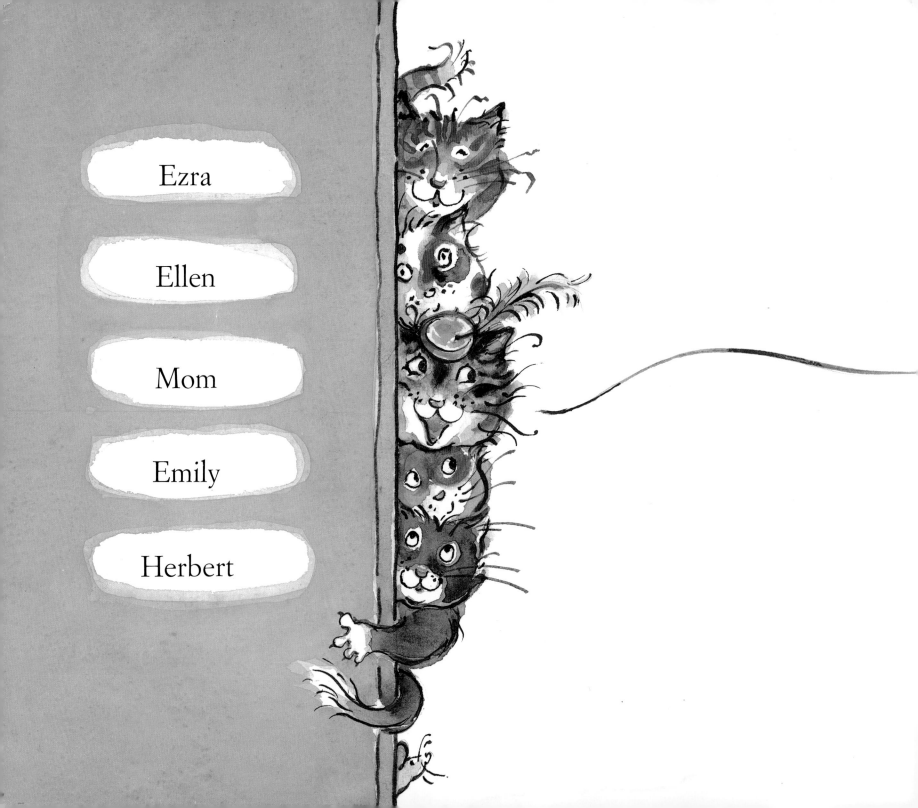

Ezra

Ellen

Mom

Emily

Herbert

# Back Soon

Diana Hendry

*illustrated by*

Carol Thompson

BridgeWater Books

For Julie, with love, Diana
For Maureen and the boys, Carol

Text copyright © 1993 by Diana Hendry.
Illustrations copyright © 1993 by Carol Thompson.

First published in Great Britain in 1993 by Julia MacRae,
an imprint of Random House,
20 Vauxhall Bridge Road, London SW1V 2SA.

Published in the United States by BridgeWater Books,
an imprint of Troll Associates, Inc.

Printed in the United States of America.

10 9 8 7 6 5 4 3 2 1

*Library of Congress Cataloging-in-Publication Data*

Hendry, Diana (date)
Back soon / by Diana Hendry; illustrated by Carol Thompson.
p.    cm.
"First published in Great Britain in 1993 by Julia MacRae, an
imprint of Random House"—T.p. verso.
Summary:  A kitten does not like it when his mother goes away
without him, but after enjoying some time by himself, he understands
why she does it.
ISBN 0-8167-3487-9 (lib. bdg.)    ISBN 0-8167-3488-7 (pbk.)
[1. Cats – Fiction.   2. Mother and child – Fiction.]   I. Thompson,
Carol, ill.   II. Title.
PZ7.H38586Bac    1995
[E] - dc20                                                                93-45590

There was only one thing wrong with
Herbert's mother.  Sometimes she would
go out without him.  Whenever she did,
she always said the same thing.
"Back soon!" she said and gave
him a loving cuff on the ear
with her paw.

"Back soon!" she said when she went down to the corner store for something she had forgotten. She left Uncle Ezra to look after him and she was back in five minutes.

"Back soon!" she said when she went to have her whiskers curled at the whisker dressers and was gone for hours and Big Sister Emily looked after him and wouldn't play Chase-the-Yarn-Spool.

"Back soon!" she said when she went into town to buy
herself a new dress and was gone the whole day and bossy
Aunt Ellen made him eat all his mouse tails.

And "Back soon!" she said when she and his father, Edward, went off for a whole weekend to see distant relatives. They said they needed a vacation. Aunt Ellen, Uncle Ezra, and Big Sister Emily all looked after him.

One day Herbert decided it was *his* turn. When his mother was ironing the pillowcases, Herbert said, "I'm going under the table now. Back soon!"

Herbert stayed under the table for five whole minutes. His mother kept on ironing. She didn't seem to miss him at all.

Herbert tried again. "I'm going up to my room now," he said. "Back soon!" His mother was cooking supper. "Don't be long," she said. "Supper's nearly ready."

Herbert stayed in his room for ten whole minutes,
twiddling his paws. It was very boring. When he came
downstairs, his mother said, "You're just in time.
Supper's ready."

The next morning was sunny and windy. "I'm going out into the garden," said Herbert very importantly to his mother. And over his shoulder, when he reached the kitchen door, "Back soon!"

It was so nice in the garden that Herbert forgot he had said he would be back soon. He pretended he was an acrobat on a branch of the lilac tree. Then he chased a stick that kept running away from him. He was just making himself nicely dizzy chasing his own tail when he heard a very sad voice coming from the open kitchen door.

"Oh, where is my Herbert?" cried this voice. "He said he'd be back soon and he's been gone for hours and I'm very lonely and I miss him terribly!"

Herbert stopped chasing his tail, stood up, and ran into the kitchen and into his mother's arms. "I'm back! I'm back!" he cried. "Did you miss me?"

"Oh, I really did!" said his mother. "But it's very nice having some time to yourself, isn't it?"

"It is," agreed Herbert, "as long as you always remember to come back."
"I always will," said his mother.
"So will I," said Herbert.